This book belongs to:

Sunshine room

A catalogue record for this book is available from the British Library

Published by Ladybird Books Ltd
A Penguin Company
Penguin Books Ltd, 80 Strand, London WC2R 0RL, UK
Penguin Books Australia Ltd, Camberwell, Victoria, Australia
Penguin Group (NZ) Ltd, 67 Apollo Drive, Rosedale, North Shore 0632, New Zealand

8 10 9 7
© LADYBIRD BOOKS LTD MCMXCVIII. This edition MMVI

ISBN-13: 978-1-84646-069-2

Printed in China

The
Three Billy
Goats Gruff

illustrated by Graham Percy

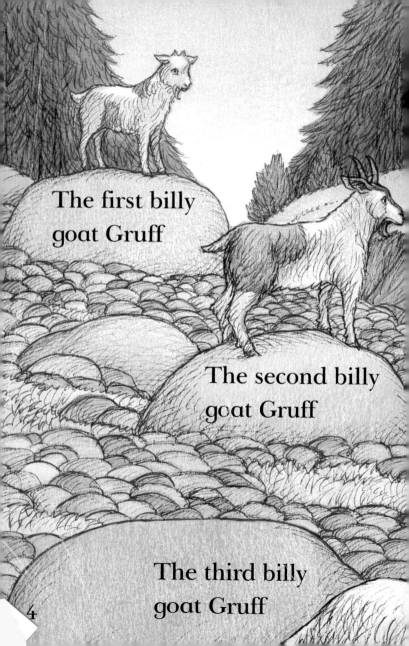

The first billy
goat Gruff

The second billy
goat Gruff

The third billy
goat Gruff

4

The troll

The grass

The bridge

5

"I'm hungry," said the first billy goat Gruff.

"I'm going over the bridge to eat the grass."

6

Trip, trap!

Trip, trap!

Trip, trap!

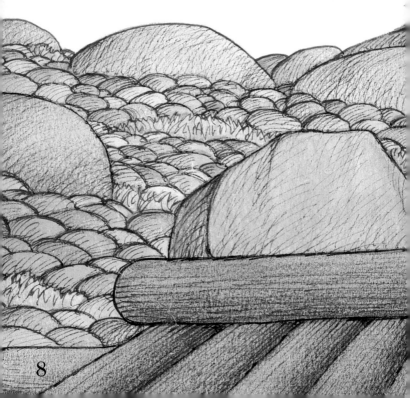

Up jumped the troll.
"I'm going to eat
you up," said
the troll.

"Oh, no," said the
first billy goat Gruff.

"Don't eat me.
Eat the second
billy goat Gruff.
He's big and fat."

12

"I'm hungry," said the second billy goat Gruff.

"I'm going over the bridge to eat the grass."

Trip, trap

Trip, trap

Trip, trap

Up jumped the troll.

"I'm going to eat
you up," said
the troll.

"Oh, no," said the second billy goat Gruff.

"Don't eat me. Eat the third billy goat Gruff. He's big and fat."

"I'm hungry," said the third billy goat Gruff.

"I'm going over the bridge to eat the grass."

Trip, trap

Trip, trap

Trip, trap

Up jumped the troll.
"I'm going to eat
you up," said
the troll.

"Oh, no, you're not," said the third billy goat Gruff.

"I'm going to eat **you** up."

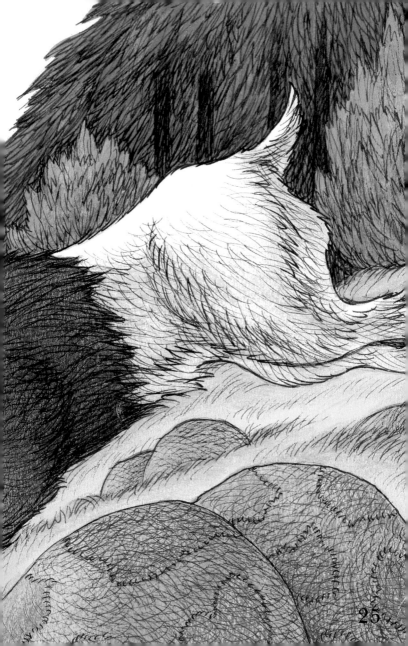

And that was the end of the troll!

Read It Yourself is a series of graded readers designed to give young children a confident and successful start to reading.

Level 1 is suitable for children who are making their first attempts at reading. The stories are told in a very simple way using a small number of frequently repeated words. The sentences on each page are closely supported by pictures to help with reading, and to offer lively details to talk about.

About this book

The pictures in this book are designed to encourage children to talk about the story and predict what might happen next.

The opening page shows a detailed scene which introduces the main characters and vocabulary appearing in the story.

After a discussion of the pictures, children can listen to an adult read the story or attempt to read it themselves. Unknown words can be worked out by looking at the beginning letter *(what sound does this letter make?)*, and deciding which word would make sense.

Beginner readers need plenty of encouragement.